For my pesky little sisters,
Becky and Jess, with love

Atheneum Books for Young Readers

An imprint of Simon & Schuster Children's Publishing Division

1230 Avenue of the Americas, New York, New York 10020

Copyright © 2007 by Sam Lloyd

First published in 2007 by Orchard Books, a Division of Watts Publishing Group Ltd., London

All rights reserved, including the right of reproduction in whole or in part in any form.

The text for this book is set in Steam.

Manufactured in China

First U. S. edition 2008

2 4 6 8 10 9 7 5 3 1

CIP data for this book is available from the Library of Congress.

ISBN-13: 978-1-4169-5796-6

ISBN-10: 1-4169-5796-0

Mr. Pusskins ♡

and Little Whiskers

another love story

Written and illustrated by

sam lloyd

Atheneum Books for Young Readers

New York   London   Toronto   Sydney

This is the story of a little girl called Emily and her dear cat, Mr. Pusskins.

Dum diddley dum dum, doo doo doo,
Sharing magic moments, just us two.

They thought life couldn't get any better.

Then, one day, Emily announced that she had a fabulous surprise for Mr. Pusskins. He was **very** excited.

Emily fetched a large cardboard box, and inside the box was ...

...a kitten!

"This is Little Whiskers,"
said Emily. "She has come to
live with us. She is only a
tiny kitten, so we need
to take care of her."

"I'm sure you two will be the best of friends," smiled Emily, "so I'll leave you to play lovely games together."

Mr. Pusskins needed to be alone.

He was somewhat disappointed with his "**fabulous surprise**," and he certainly wasn't in the mood for "**lovely games.**"

Little Whiskers wasn't in the mood
for **lovely games** either....

The pesky kitten took great delight in ruining all Mr. Pusskins' special times.

She ruined telly time...

she ruined meal time...

she ruined play time...

she ruined nap time . . .

How to relax
S. LLOYD

When Emily wasn't
looking, Little Whiskers ruined

EVERYTHING!

Mr. Pusskins could bear it no longer.
Something had to be done.

So, that evening, Mr. Pusskins wrote a letter.

To whom it may concern,

I am displeased with my "fabulous surprise." I find the kitten EXTREMELY irritating and wish to return her ASAP.

Yours fed-up-ingly,

Mr. P.

Tomorrow he would send it!

Then Mr. Pusskins
settled down for
a nice long sleep. . . .

BAM
BAM

Suddenly a hideous
noise woke him.
He dashed to
see what was
going on. . . .

CLUNK CLUNK

Emily dashed too. And who did she see? "Mr. Pusskins!" she gasped. "You know better than to play such a terrible tune at this time of night. You might have woken Little Whiskers!"

Emily banished Mr. Pusskins outside. "You need to think about what you've done wrong," she said.

But Mr. Pusskins hadn't done anything wrong. As rain turned to snow, he thought about his cozy home.

He reached up to the window to take
a peek. . . . That wretched kitten! She was
already sitting in Mr. Pusskins' favorite
spot by the fireside. Mr. Pusskins was

FURIOUS!

But Little Whiskers wasn't
enjoying the fireside. She knew
she had been behaving naughtily,
not Mr. Pusskins.

How she wished there was a way she could
make things better. And there was. . . .

Little Whiskers leapt onto the piano. . . .

BAM BAM
CLUNK CLUNK
BOOM BOOM BOOM

In rushed Emily. "Oh, good gracious!"
she gasped. "Little Whiskers! It was
you that played that
terrible tune,
wasn't it?!"

"Miaow," admitted
the kitten.

Emily hurried outside. "My poor Mr. Pusskins!
Please forgive me," she begged.
And, of course, Mr. Pusskins did.

Little Whiskers
asked Mr. Pusskins
to forgive her too.

And eventually...

Mr. Pusskins
DID!

Mr. Pusskins didn't send the letter after all. He decided Little Whiskers could stay.

This is the end of the story of a little girl called Emily and her dear cats, Mr. Pusskins and Little Whiskers.

Dum diddley dum dum, dee dee dee,
Sharing magic moments, just us three!

And now
life is perfect!